The Whipping Man

by Matthew Lopez

D1563570

A SAMUEL FRENCH ACTING EDITION

SAMUEL FRENCH

FOUNDED 1830

New York Hollywood London Toronto

SAMUELFRENCH.COM

ISBN 978-0-573-69709-8   Printed in U.S.A.   #29121

**IMPORTANT BILLING AND CREDIT
REQUIREMENTS**

All producers of *THE WHIPPING MAN must* give credit to the Author of the Play in all programs distributed in connection with performances of the Play, and in all instances in which the title of the Play appears for the purposes of advertising, publicizing or otherwise exploiting the Play and/or a production. The name of the Author *must* appear on a separate line on which no other name appears, immediately following the title and *must* appear in size of type not less than fifty percent of the size of the title type.

THE WHIPPING MAN was originally produced by The Luna Stage Company (Jane Mandel, Artistic Director) in Montclair, New Jersey, April 29, 2006, under the direction of Linnet Taylor with the following cast and production staff:

Simon..Frankie R. Faison
Caleb...Douglas Scott Sorenson
John..Brandon O'Neil Scott

Paul Whelihan – Stage Manager
Amanda Embry – Scenic Design
Colleen Kesterson – Costume Design
Jill Nagle – Lighting Design
Margaret Pine – Sound Design

THE WHIPPING MAN was produced by the Penumbra Theatre Company (Lou Bellamy, Artistic Director) in St. Paul, Minnesota, February 19, 2009, under the direction of Lou Bellamy with the following cast and production staff:

Simon...……James Craven
Caleb..Joseph Papke
John..Duane Boutté

Mary Winchell – Stage Manager
Kenneth F. Evans – Scenic Design
Kalere A. Payton – Costume Design
Kathy A. Perkins – Lighting Design
Martin Gwinup – Sound Design

CHARACTERS

SIMON – 50s, former slave in the DeLeon home
CALEB – 20s, only child of the DeLeon family
JOHN – 20s, former slave in the DeLeon home

SETTING

The ruins of a once grand home in Richmond, Virginia.

Scene 1: Late night, April 13, 1865
Scene 2: Morning, April 14, 1865
Scene 3: Evening, April 14, 1865
Scene 4: Evening, April 15, 1865

PERFORMANCE NOTE

I've seen the play performed with and without an intermission. Both seem to work just fine. If you feel the need to have one, the best place is after Scene 3.

–Matthew Lopez

AUTHOR'S NOTE

Several books were infinitely helpful in my research for this play and they might be helpful for any production. For information on Judaism in antebellum south, I relied on Robert N. Rosen's *The Jewish Confederates* and Bertram Korn's *American Jewry and the Civil War*. For descriptions of urban slave-owning, I turned to Frederick Douglass' *My Bondage and My Freedom*. Finally, *April 1865: The Month That Saved America* by Jay Winik and *Richmond Burning*" by Nelson Lankford served as the basis for my depiction of Richmond in the days following the end of the war.

–*Matthew Lopez*
2009

For my parents, who never doubted.

Scene One

(Richmond, Virginia. Thursday, April 13, 1865. Around ten o'clock at night.)

(The lights rise on what was once the front entrance of a grand town home, now in ruins. Craters dot the hardwood floors. The wallpaper is stained with soot and parts of it are burned away. Most of the windows are broken. The railing of the grand staircase leans perilously down to the floor, as if it would collapse with the slightest touch. The steps themselves are broken and jagged. The damage to the house suggests recent destruction rather than years of neglect. This was someone's home not too long ago. But it is now a haunted house.)

(A violent thunderstorm is raging outside. At the crack of a thunderbolt, the front door swings open. A **YOUNG MAN** *in a tattered Confederate Captain's uniform leans against the doorway. He is bearded, thin and dirty. He hops on one leg toward the center of the room. He then slowly extends his other leg and tries to put weight on it. He lets out a cry of pain and collapses onto the floor in a dead faint.)*

(A few moments pass. Slowly, an **OLDER MAN** *enters from the kitchen. He is middle-aged, black. He carries a shotgun with a lantern dangling from the end. It is too dark to see anything. The* **OLDER MAN** *cautiously approaches.)*

(Lightning and thunder. The room fills with light for a brief moment. **OLDER MAN** *sees* **YOUNG MAN** *on the floor.)*

OLDER MAN. Hey, you.

Hey you, there.

(He taps the **YOUNG MAN** *with his foot. The* **YOUNG MAN** *starts to crawl away, like a frightened animal.* **OLDER MAN** *aims the rifle.)*

OLDER MAN. Don't move, Soldier.

(The **YOUNG MAN** *continues crawling as the* **OLDER MAN** *puts the rifle to the back of his head.)*

OLDER MAN. I said don't move.

*(***YOUNG MAN** *stops crawling.)*

OLDER MAN. Turn around.

(No response.)

OLDER MAN. Turn around.

(The **YOUNG MAN** *slowly and painfully turns. As he does:)*

OLDER MAN. They ain't nothing left to steal here, if that's what you're thinkin'. If it's dying you're looking to do, you best do that elsewhere.

(The **YOUNG MAN** *is now on his back. He looks up at the* **OLDER MAN**.*)*

YOUNG MAN. Simon? Simon, is that you?

(The **OLDER MAN** *looks down at the* **YOUNG MAN**'s *face.)*

SIMON. Caleb?

CALEB. Yes. Oh, God. Am I home? Is this…am I home?

SIMON. You are.

CALEB. I'm home?

SIMON. Yes.

CALEB. God. God, oh, God…

*(***CALEB** *sinks to the floor.)*

*(***SIMON** *kneels down and touches his head.)*

SIMON. *Hagomel le'chayavim tovim she'gmalani kol tov.* Amen.

(Silence a moment, then **SIMON** *stands and moves to the window. He takes out a handkerchief and wipes a layer of grime off the sill. He looks back at* **CALEB**.*)*

SIMON. I been trying to clean up as best I could. Sometimes I think there's no point and I just give up. But I always start up again.

(SIMON begins lighting the few lamps that are in the room. CALEB sits up, only now seeing the devastation.)

CALEB. My God, look at this place. I wasn't even sure I was in the right house when I rode up. What happened?

SIMON. This house? Fire and rain did most of the work. Been raining for days. Whole town looks like this.

CALEB. I saw.

SIMON. Looting, stealing. That done it, too.

CALEB. The Yanks?

SIMON. Some. Some not. Slaves from around. Poor whites from around. Hell happened to this house. Looks like hell done happened to you, too.

CALEB. Where are my folks?

SIMON. Gone.

CALEB. Where?

SIMON. Your ma's gone to Williamsburg to be with your grandmother. Your pa left with President Davis and the rest of the Cabinet.

CALEB. Where'd they go?

SIMON. Who knows?

CALEB. Who does know?

SIMON. Not me.

CALEB. And Sarah?

SIMON. What about Sarah?

CALEB. Is she here?

SIMON. Your pa took her and Lizbeth with him when he left with the President.

CALEB. When will they be back?

SIMON. Soon, God willing.

CALEB. You're here all alone?

SIMON. I am.

CALEB. What about…?

SIMON. Haven't seen him for weeks. Probably on a drunk somewhere.

CALEB. Or gone.

SIMON. I'd bet money on a bottle before I'd bet on him leaving.

CALEB. You been here by yourself this whole time?

SIMON. Only recently. 'Fore this, I was up at the soldier's hospital with your ma and the women from the temple.

CALEB. Nursing?

SIMON. Nursing, bandaging, takin' off limbs. Whatever needed doing. Then when the Federals came, your ma left for Williamsburg…

CALEB. …and told you to come here and wait for everybody.

SIMON. She asked me.

(pause)

CALEB. Oh. Yes.

(CALEB tries to get up. It's no good.)

SIMON. You wounded?

CALEB. Just grazed.

SIMON. When?

CALEB. Week. Maybe more?

SIMON. Them Federal doctors didn't clean it?

CALEB. What Federal doctors?

SIMON. When you surrendered.

CALEB. No.

No, they…they were more concerned with their own, I guess.

SIMON. We'd best take a look at it. Might need to take you to the soldier's hospital.

CALEB. It's not that bad.

SIMON. Week-old wounds have a habit of killing people. Best let me take a look at it.

(SIMON pulls out a pocketknife and cuts CALEB's pant leg open at the knee to reveal a rotting bullet wound.)

SIMON. God in heaven. This ain't no graze. This is a bullet hole. You was shot a week ago and you ain't had it cleaned?

CALEB. It was chaos.

SIMON. We need to clean this. Your pa has some whiskey left.

CALEB. Some? He has cases…

SIMON. Had cases.

(SIMON moves to a section of the torn-up floorboards and begins reaching under.)

CALEB. Where'd all the whiskey go?

SIMON. Same place it always goes when they's trouble.

(He mimes chugging at a bottle. Then he finds a whiskey bottle.)

SIMON. Here she is.

(SIMON moves back to CALEB and opens the bottle.)

SIMON. This is gonna hurt, now.

CALEB. I'm sure I've felt worse.

(SIMON pours the whiskey on the wound.)

CALEB. Jesus Christ, Simon, that hurts!

(CALEB grabs the bottle and takes a healthy swig. SIMON takes the bottle back and continues to pour the remainder of the whiskey over the wound while examining him.)

SIMON. You say you rode here?

CALEB. I had a horse.

SIMON. Had?

CALEB. Dead. Out front.

SIMON. Just as well. Can't feed a horse, anyway. Could eat one, though. That horse have any meat on him?

CALEB. Some. He spent a week dying.

SIMON. Well, if he does have some, we're gonna eat it. He ain't got no need for it no more and God knows we could use a meal.

CALEB. Yes.

SIMON. I've got rags in the kitchen. I need to clean this wound.

(*SIMON exits to the kitchen.* **CALEB** *grabs the bottle and tries to get a few drops into his mouth.*)

(*A figure is seen moving around on the front porch, looking through the windows.*)

CALEB. Who's there? Who is that?

(*The figure moves away.*)

CALEB. Simon! Simon, get in here!

(**SIMON** *re-enters.*)

SIMON. What? What is it?

CALEB. Something was moving out there, looking in the windows.

(**SIMON** *grabs the rifle and the lantern and moves to the front door. He opens the door and looks about. No one is there. He comes back into the house.*)

SIMON. No one there.

CALEB. There was someone looking through the window.

SIMON. Well, if they take a look again, it'll be down the barrel of this shotgun.

(**SIMON** *continues to look out the window for a moment then turns to face* **CALEB.***)

SIMON. You ain't gonna like what I'm about to say.

CALEB. What?

SIMON. Your leg, it…you got the gangrene pretty bad.

CALEB. How bad?

SIMON. It ain't gone above the knee, which is good, but… that leg gonna haveta come off.

(*pause*)

CALEB. No. No way in hell.

SIMON. You ain't got no choice.

CALEB. No!

SIMON. You're gonna die if we don't.

CALEB. I saw what it was like when they took off those limbs, Simon. I can't go through that. I won't. I'd rather die.

SIMON. You will. As sure as I'm here lookin' at you, you will die. And it's an awful death. We don't cut that leg off at the knee, the gangrene gonna keep crawling right up your leg, hurting every inch as it does. It gonna pass through your privates. They gonna fall off like ripe apples on a tree. They gonna be a big hole where your Tommy Johnson used to be. It gonna eat away at your liver, your stomach, your kidneys. It gonna crawl right up to your heart and turn it black. Blacker than my fist. Your blood gonna be so filled with poison, every part of you is gonna hurt. You gonna be in more pain than you ever thought you could stand. You gonna lose your mind with the pain. And then...and only then... will you die. The pain you gonna feel having this leg come off today gonna feel like a tickle compared to the pain you gonna feel when you die of poisoned blood on Sunday. You understand me?

CALEB. If I do this, I'm gonna be better?

SIMON. You gonna have a chance of being better. I wouldn't be saying this if I didn't believe it. Do you trust me?

(**CALEB** *signals his acquiescence by lying back down.*)

SIMON. Good. Now, I need to clean this wound and then find some help in the morning to take you to the soldier's hospital.

CALEB. No! No hospital. Do it here.

SIMON. I can't.

CALEB. If you think this is something I need, then you're gonna do it.

SIMON. I can't.

CALEB. Yes you can. You've done it before, haven't you?

SIMON. Not by myself. I could kill you.

CALEB. I'd rather die on this floor than at that hospital. I'd rather you kill me then some Federal doctor.

SIMON. I can't do it.

CALEB. You will. You got tools?

SIMON. I got what I need.

CALEB. How much whiskey we have left?

SIMON. Not enough to keep the wound clean and get you as drunk as you're gonna need to be.

CALEB. How drunk?

SIMON. Dead drunk. Even that ain't gonna be enough.

CALEB. We'll make do with what we've got. Go look for more whiskey. Find what you can. Check the cellar.

SIMON. Caleb?

CALEB. What?

SIMON. All these things you're telling me to do, by rights now you need to be asking me to do.

CALEB. Are you asking me to chop my leg off or are you telling me?

SIMON. I'm telling you.

CALEB. Then I'm telling you to go get the fuckin' whiskey. If you're giving orders, I'm giving orders. That sound fair to you?

SIMON. Fair enough for now.

CALEB. Go.

(**SIMON** *exits.*)

(*The figure appears again at the window.*)

CALEB. Who's there? Who is that?

(*The figure moves to the door.*)

CALEB. Who are you?

(*The front door slowly opens. We see the figure standing in the shadows. He wears a cloth hood over his face with two eye holes cut out, putting him in likeness of an executioner. He exudes menace.*)

MAN. Captain Caleb DeLeon?

CALEB. Who is that?

MAN. Are you Captain Caleb DeLeon?

CALEB. Who are you?

MAN. I am the man asking if you are Captain Caleb DeLeon.

CALEB. What do you want?

MAN. I have a message for you.

CALEB. From who?

> *(No answer.)*

CALEB. What is the message?

> *(A moment, then the MAN rips the hood off to reveal the face of JOHN, a young black man close to Caleb's age.)*

JOHN. Nigger John has come home!

> *(JOHN laughs with glee and dances around, delighted with himself. It's a "boo! I gotchya" moment that JOHN performs with devilish relish. CALEB jumps at this then, knowing he is safe, relaxes.)*

> *(About JOHN's appearance: he is feral. His clothes are dirty and tattered. His feet are bare. His hair is grown out and a week's worth of beard sits on his face. He also has a cloth bandage wrapped around one hand.)*

CALEB. Jesus, John, you scared me half to death.

JOHN. You look at least to be three-quarters there.
This your dead horse here?

CALEB. Yeah.

JOHN. I don't know which of the two of you looks worse.

> *(JOHN looks behind him as if checking to see that the coast is clear, then he steps inside and closes the door.)*

CALEB. Was that you creepin' around just then?

JOHN. I saw a soldier crawling up to the house and thought he might be up to no good.

CALEB. I thought you were a looter.

JOHN. I was havin' the same thoughts about you.

CALEB. Good to know the house is well-protected.

JOHN. Not that there's all that much left to protect.

(He moves into the room, looking around.)

JOHN. Just you and Simon, then?

CALEB. That's right.

JOHN. No one else?

CALEB. You.

> *(**JOHN** looks **CALEB** over.)*

JOHN. You wounded?

CALEB. Yeah.

JOHN. Bad?

CALEB. No.
Where've you been? Simon says you've been missing.

JOHN. I didn't miss a thing.

CALEB. You've been in Richmond?

JOHN. I have.

CALEB. What's the news? Have you heard anything?

JOHN. I've heard everything. Same thing you've heard, I imagine. War's over. You lost. We won.
Whiskey?

CALEB. What?

JOHN. You want some whiskey?

(He reaches into his sack and pulls out a full bottle of whiskey.)

CALEB. Where in hell did you get that?

JOHN. A neighbor.

CALEB. You stole it. I knew you've been stealing.

JOHN. I didn't steal anything. "Stealing" is when someone has gone to great lengths to protect something. That was not the case with this, although there was a case of this. The house was half burned and the doors were wide open. No, this whiskey was liberated and is now being occupied by me.

(He takes a drink then holds it out to **CALEB**.*)*

JOHN. Want some?

*(***CALEB*** stares at the bottle for a moment then reluctantly gestures for it. ***JOHN*** hands it to him and ***CALEB*** begins drinking.)*

JOHN. You were in Petersburg?

CALEB. I was.

JOHN. Was it as bad as they say?

CALEB. How bad did they say?

JOHN. That it weren't no tea party.

CALEB. No. It was not.

JOHN. You surrendered with them at Appomattox?

CALEB. I did.

JOHN. That must've stung.

CALEB. It is what it is.

JOHN. Yes, it is.

(They sit a moment in silence, passing the bottle between each other.)

JOHN. What do I call you now?

CALEB. Call me?

JOHN. "Master" doesn't quite fit anymore.

CALEB. You never called me that.

JOHN. "Sir?" Do I address you as "sir," now?

CALEB. You never called me that, either. I think "Caleb" will be just fine.

JOHN. Will he?

*(***SIMON*** has entered, unnoticed, carrying a toolbox and a bottle of whiskey.)*

SIMON. Where you been, boy?

JOHN. Simon.

*(***JOHN*** approaches him. ***SIMON*** pulls him out of earshot from ***CALEB***, who nurses the whiskey.)*

SIMON. Where you been?

JOHN. Here, there. Mostly there. This place sure got picked over.

SIMON. You have anything to do with it?

JOHN. I wish I had.

SIMON. I needed you here and you just up and disappeared.

JOHN. Well, now I just up and re-appeared.

SIMON. What'd you do to your hand?

JOHN. It's nothing.

SIMON. Let me take a look at it.

JOHN. I said it's nothing. Just a cut, that's all.
    What's Caleb's ailment?

SIMON. Bullet wound in his leg.

JOHN. He says it's not bad.

SIMON. He ain't a doctor.

JOHN. Neither are you.

SIMON. Closest thing he got to one. It's gonna haveta come off.

JOHN. Does he know that?

SIMON. He ain't got no choice. I've been trying to get him to go to the hospital but he won't budge.

JOHN. So...what, then?

SIMON. Well, I told him I'd do it here but it's too much for one man, especially in the dark. I figured if I started laying out all my tools it might scare him into going to the hospital. If that don't work, I just figured to get him drunk. He's half starved as it is. It won't take much for him to pass out. Then we take him to the hospital, whether he wants to go or not.

JOHN. We?

SIMON. I need your help, John.

JOHN. Let me ask you something...given all that's happened, given that we're not slaves anymore...how is this our problem?

SIMON. Our problem? That boy is dying. Layin' on his mama's floor and dying. That's a problem.

JOHN. Could we do it here? If I helped...could you...could we do it?

SIMON. Could do, but...it ain't an easy thing. He's going to be kicking and screaming. You think you're strong enough to hold him down?

JOHN. I've been strong enough to do that since we were kids. So how do we do this, then? You just chop it with an axe or something?

SIMON. An axe? You crazy, boy?

JOHN. Well, I don't know! I've never taken off someone's leg before.

SIMON. We use a saw. Saw at his leg right above the knee. Here, see?

(He points to a spot on JOHN's leg. He continues to explain using JOHN's leg as an example.)

SIMON. We gotta cut through the skin, through the muscle, right down to the bone.

JOHN. And then?

SIMON. Then? Clear through the bone. As fast as we can. He's gonna be wiggling and struggling. The more he struggles, the harder it's gonna be for me to cut.

(JOHN grabs the whiskey from SIMON and takes a huge gulp.)

SIMON. Through the bone, onto the other side of the leg. The muscle, the skin. Till it comes right off.

JOHN. That's it, then?

SIMON. That's just the beginning. He's got an artery there in his leg. Got to tie that off or else he gonna bleed to death. As it is, he gonna be bleeding all over hisself and us, too.

JOHN. You know how to tie it off?

SIMON. Done it hundreds of times. Then we take the skin from his leg and we cut it, we pull it back. Like pulling the husk off of corn, see? And we cut away at the muscle on the leg 'til the bone's sticking out. We wrap the skin around the bone. We fold them, one over the other and sew it up. That makes the stump, see?

JOHN. He's awake during all this?

SIMON. Depends on his strength. Some men pass out at the sight of the saw. Others watch the whole thing.

JOHN. And what about the person holding him down? When does he usually pass out?

SIMON. I need you strong, John.

JOHN. I can do this.

SIMON. It ain't gonna be pretty. We gonna be up all night.

JOHN. So, then…let's get started.

(**JOHN** *takes a healthy swig and offers the bottle to* **SIMON**, *who declines a drink.* **JOHN** *corks the bottle and hands it back to* **SIMON**. **SIMON** *goes to* **CALEB** *with the bottle, leaving the toolbox behind.*)

SIMON. All right, Caleb. We're gonna do things your way. We won't take you to the hospital but we got to do this now. Keep drinking.

CALEB. Goddamn, Simon, I'm already drunk.

SIMON. Drink. Big ol' gulps. Go on.

CALEB. Simon, I–

SIMON. You shoulda had the wound cleaned days ago. You shoulda had that leg off by now.

CALEB. Simon, I think I changed my mind.

SIMON. You want to go to the hospital?

CALEB. No.

SIMON. Then you ain't got no mind to change. You best start drinking that whiskey. Your bottle is for your belly. My bottle is for your leg. If I finish my bottle before you finish yours, you gonna be in a world a hurt.

(**CALEB** *hesitates then begins quickly drinking.*)

JOHN. Jesus, Caleb! Didn't they teach you any manners in the Army?

SIMON. Keep drinking.

(**SIMON** *motions to* **JOHN** *for a chair.*)

CALEB. Simon, I think I'm going to be sick.

SIMON. You gonna be a lot sicker if we don't get this leg off. Drink.

(JOHN *hands* SIMON *the chair and* SIMON *sets it on its side.* CALEB *continues drinking.*)

CALEB. Simon–

SIMON. Keep drinking.

I'm gonna grab your leg, now.

(SIMON *grabs* CALEB *by his leg and* JOHN *takes him by the shoulders. They move him over to the chair and rest his leg on it.* SIMON *rips* CALEB*'s pant leg open to above the knee.* CALEB*'s leg is rotting. As this is happening...*)

CALEB. Simon, I don't want you to do this.

SIMON. Got no choice, Caleb.

CALEB. Simon, I don't want you to.

SIMON. You gonna die if we don't.

CALEB. Simon, I'm scared.

SIMON. I know you scared.

CALEB. Simon, it's gonna hurt.

SIMON. Gonna hurt real bad, yes.

(SIMON *takes the bottle and pours the whiskey over the wound.* CALEB *screams and tries to get away.* SIMON *stops him.*)

SIMON. John! You gotta hold him down, now. Hold him down.

(JOHN *pins* CALEB *to the floor.* SIMON *repositions* CALEB*'s leg on the chair.* CALEB *struggles against* JOHN.)

(SIMON *goes to the tool box and pulls out a saw.* CALEB *sees it.*)

CALEB. No!

(JOHN *struggles to keep* CALEB *pinned.* SIMON *returns and holds down both of* CALEB*'s legs as best he can while also positioning the saw onto* CALEB*'s leg. Throughout this:*)

CALEB. Simon, no. No, please, Simon. Don't do this.

SIMON. Got no choice, Caleb.

CALEB. Simon, please, please don't do this.

SIMON. It needs doing, Caleb.

CALEB. PLEASEDON'TDOTHISPLEASEDON'TDOTHISP
LEASEDON'TDOTHISPLEASEDON'TDOTHIS...

SIMON. Hold him tight, now, John.

JOHN. He's not going anywhere.

CALEB. DON'TDOTHISDON'TDOTHISDON'TDOTHIS!
DON'T YOU FUCKING DO THIS!
DON'T YOU FUCKING DO THIS!
DON'TYOUFUCKINGNO!

(**SIMON** *pulls the saw back, making the first cut into*
CALEB*'s leg. The lights immediately fade on them and*
slowly rise on the rest of the house. It is our first full look
at the ruin. **CALEB** *screams. It is as if his screams were*
pushing the light upward. His screams echo throughout
the empty house as the lights finally fade completely.)

End of Scene One

Scene Two

(The next morning. Friday, April 14, 1865.)

(The rain continues.)

*(***CALEB*** is sleeping on a mattress on the floor. His leg is gone and he is covered in quilts and blankets. A few sacks filled with pilfered goods lay around the room. Stacks of books are scattered around, as well.)*

*(***SIMON*** sits on the floor with a bucket and a scrub brush, cleaning the bloodstains. A cup of what we take to be coffee sits steaming by his side.)*

*(***JOHN*** enters from upstairs, carrying a sack. He is dressed in better clothes than in Scene 1. He trudges down and sits on the foot of the stairs, watching ***SIMON*** scrubbing. After a moment…)*

JOHN. That coffee?

SIMON. Water. Ain't no coffee.

JOHN. You're just drinking hot water?

SIMON. It warms me.

JOHN. Wouldn't you rather have coffee?

SIMON. I'd rather have flapjacks and some eggs. Some toast, maybe, with some jam. I'd rather have some of Lizbeth's country fried chicken with the thick, white gravy she put on it. And while we're at it, I'd rather have a soft feather bed to lay down in and have the first decent night's sleep I've had in years. And when I've had all that, then, yes, I wouldn't mind a nice cup of hot coffee.

*(He goes back to scrubbing. ***JOHN*** rummages through his sack and pulls out a smaller sack of coffee and tosses it over to ***SIMON***. ***SIMON*** opens it and smells deeply.)*

SIMON. Where'd you get this?

JOHN. Found it.

SIMON. Stole it.

JOHN. Found, stole. What's the difference? Course, if you have an objection, I can always…

(He reaches for the coffee but **SIMON** *moves it away from him.)*

JOHN. Guess you wouldn't be interested in these, either...

(He pulls a handful of eggs from his coat pocket.)

SIMON. You "found" those, too?

JOHN. These, I "discovered."

SIMON. You best be careful you don't discover yourself staring down the business end of a shotgun.

JOHN. All these houses are deserted.

SIMON. This one ain't.

JOHN. Most of them are. It's like they unlocked the doors of a store and said "welcome."

SIMON. Yeah, but folks will be coming back to these houses eventually. A couple of eggs ain't nobody gonna miss. But them duds you got on...

JOHN. You survive your way, I'll survive mine.

(He reaches into his sack and pulls out a bottle of whiskey.)

SIMON. It ain't barely even noon.

JOHN. I know. I do believe I am behind schedule.

*(***JOHN*** *looks over at* **CALEB.***)*

JOHN. How's Prince Caleb?

SIMON. Still out cold. He's been runnin' a fever this morning. I'm hoping it'll break soon. He lost a lot of blood.

JOHN. I don't want to see anything like that ever again.

SIMON. You'll be a lucky man if you don't. We need to keep an eye on him next few days. You best save some of that whiskey for him once he wakes up.

JOHN. Don't worry about the whiskey. I guarantee we won't run out.

(pause)

SIMON. What you got planned for yourself, John?

JOHN. Me? I figure I'll finish this bottle, maybe start a new book. Looking forward to dinner...

SIMON. I mean with your life.

JOHN. Oh.

SIMON. Mr. DeLeon ever talk to you about money?

JOHN. Mr. DeLeon never talked to me about anything.

SIMON. Before the war ended, he told me he was gonna give us money if we was freed.

JOHN. Bullshit.

SIMON. He said.

JOHN. He never told me.

SIMON. He only told me once.

JOHN. Maybe he was drunk.

SIMON. He was sober as a glass of water.

JOHN. How much?

SIMON. Enough.

JOHN. When?

SIMON. When he gets back. Like he done with Bad Eye, remember?

JOHN. No.

SIMON. Bad Eye bought hisself free and Mr. DeLeon bought his train ticket up North. Gave him some pocket money to get started. Bad Eye went to New York City with Mr. DeLeon's help.

JOHN. That's what you're here for?

SIMON. That and I'm waiting for Lizbeth and Sarah to come home.

(JOHN *takes a swig.*)

JOHN. How do you know he'll keep his word?

SIMON. I don't. If he doesn't, we're no worse off than we are now.

JOHN. Which isn't saying much. That's why you're so keen to help out old Caleb here?

SIMON. I'm doing it because it's the right thing to do. But if Mr. DeLeon comes home to find his son dead and we could have helped him…

JOHN. No money.

SIMON. That'd be the least of our troubles.

*(***SIMON*** stands.)*

SIMON. You didn't happen to discover a frying pan, did you?

JOHN. I'll keep an eye out for one.

SIMON. You best be careful.

*(***SIMON*** starts to exit.)*

JOHN. You don't have to worry about me.

SIMON. Someone needs to.

*(***SIMON*** trudges off to the kitchen. ***JOHN*** stands looking at ***CALEB***. He then goes back upstairs with his loot.)*

End of Scene Two

Scene 3

(Evening. Friday, April 14, 1865.)

(The rain continues.)

(Candles are lit around the front parlor. **CALEB** *is still asleep.)*

(Elsewhere in the house, the evidence of John's looting is even more apparent. There are some chairs, all mismatched. There are small pieces of furniture; mounds of clothing; the saddle from Caleb's horse; other things that might have been taken from neighboring houses. It is as if John were trying to repopulate the furnishings of this house piece by mismatched piece. The room is still more empty than full, but there is an obvious feeling of addition.)

*(***JOHN*** enters from upstairs, carrying two burlap sacks. He gently lays one down on the ground then walks over to* **CALEB** *and drops the sack near his head. The sound of utensils and clanging metal wakes* **CALEB** *up.* **JOHN** *pretends to play a bugle, blaring out Reveille.)*

JOHN. On your foot, soldier!

*(***JOHN*** laughs and pulls a bottle of whiskey out of his pocket, sits next to* **CALEB** *and begins drinking.)*

CALEB. You stole all this?

JOHN. Just the necessities: old chairs for firewood, candles and pillows and blankets to keep you warm.

CALEB. And the rest?

JOHN. Silverware. Very nice silverware.

CALEB. To sell.

JOHN. To eat with. We are not savages.

*(***JOHN*** takes another drink, then offers it to* **CALEB** *but makes him have to reach for it. As he does, he is seized by a bolt of pain that rips through his leg. He screams.)*

CALEB. GODDAMMIT!

JOHN. Careful there.

CALEB. GODDAMMITGODDAMMITGODDAMMIT!

JOHN. Easy, now, easy. Take another drink.

(CALEB *takes the bottle and drinks as the pain slowly
subsides.*)

JOHN. Seems funny that you didn't have that leg looked at
when you could have.

CALEB. It was chaos.

JOHN. Oh, I've no doubt. But still…

CALEB. What?

JOHN. No, it's just funny, that's all.

(JOHN *reaches for the bottle.* CALEB *hands it to him.
They pass the bottle back and forth in silence.*)

CALEB. What're you going to do when the folks who own
all this stuff come looking for it?

JOHN. I'll be long gone by then.

CALEB. Where?

JOHN. You remember Bad Eye?

CALEB. Bad Eye?

JOHN. Bad Eye was about ten years older than us. Had
that one eye that didn't work so well? Kind of rolled
around in the socket like a marble? Used to scare you.

CALEB. He never scared me.

JOHN. So you do remember him, then?

CALEB. I might.

JOHN. When he left, he told me he was heading up to
New York with money in his pockets and a train ticket
bought by your father. The day he left, Bad Eye pulls
me aside and says to me, "Nigger John…"

CALEB. He never called you that.

JOHN. Oh, he did. Your nickname caught on fast. "Nigger
John," he says, "you come up to New York when you
get free from here. You come up to New York and I'll
set you up with a job and a bed and a way to start your
life."

CALEB. That's what you're going to do?

JOHN. That is what I am going to do.

(CALEB chuckles.)

JOHN. That funny to you?

CALEB. It's pathetic to me. You know how far New York is?

JOHN. I know how far.

CALEB. You're just going to head on up to New York. Out of this town.

JOHN. The hell outta this town.

CALEB. And when you get there, how do you plan on finding him?

JOHN. I'll find him.

CALEB. Just gonna stand on every street corner in New York City, yelling out "Bad Eye, Bad Eye, where are you?"

JOHN. If that's what it takes.

CALEB. "Ten years after you left, here I am, Bad Eye."

JOHN. Enough.

CALEB. "After four years of war, here I am."

JOHN. That's enough…

CALEB. That's about he dumbest thing I ever heard.

JOHN. I SAID ENOUGH!

CALEB. You think my father is going to give you money?

JOHN. He told me he would.

CALEB. When?

JOHN. Several times. Told me, told Simon.

CALEB. Well, if that is true, it sounds like a decent thing to do.

JOHN. Seeing as I do not have the money in my hand at the present, I will refrain from making that judgment.

(JOHN moves to the kitchen and yells off…)

JOHN. Hey, Simon…when's dinner gonna be ready?

SIMON. *(off)* You keep askin' like that, the answer gonna be "never."

JOHN. Caleb's awake.

(SIMON enters from the kitchen and stops to look at him.)

SIMON. Well…you slept a good long time. Almost a full day.

CALEB. Simon, I feel something awful.

SIMON. You gonna be in pain for a while.

John, I want you to keep him in as much whiskey as you can find. That'll keep the pain at bay as best we can and keep any infection from setting in.

CALEB. How is drinkin' whiskey gonna keep an infection away?

SIMON. Shoot, whiskey'll kill anything. Killed your Uncle Charlie.

You think you can eat?

CALEB. Could try.

SIMON. I butchered that horse last night. Meat's tough but there's a lot of it.

JOHN. Horse meat isn't kosher, Simon.

SIMON. Neither is stealin' from your neighbor. You go find me a Rabbi and we'll ask him which is worse. You hungry, ain't you?

JOHN. Yeah.

SIMON. Then it's as kosher as it's gonna get for now.

(**SIMON** *heads back to the kitchen, then stops and pulls* **JOHN** *aside.*)

SIMON. Freddy Cole came around today while you was sleeping off your drunk.

(*slight pause*)

JOHN. Oh yeah? What'd he want?

SIMON. He wanted you. Say he been lookin' for you about a week now.

JOHN. What did you tell him?

SIMON. Something told me I shouldn't tell him anything. Why do you think I got that feeling?

JOHN. I don't think anyone wants Freddy Cole knowin' where he is.

SIMON. He wasn't lookin' for me, John. You do something make Freddy Cole angry?

JOHN. Doesn't take much.

SIMON. John...

JOHN. You tell Freddy Cole next time he comes round looking for me that you ain't seen me. You tell him I'm long gone and ain't never coming back. You tell him Nigger John says let bygones be bygones and to kiss my emancipated ass!

(He heads up the stairs and off. SIMON *calls after him.)*

SIMON. You done something against Freddy Cole, you got to make it right, boy! You can't run from him forever! You living in this world now, not just servin' in it!

*(*SIMON *exits to the kitchen as* JOHN *re-enters with another sack of looted goods in one hand and a fresh bottle of whiskey in the other.)*

CALEB. Freddy Cole is not the kind of man you wanna be pissin' off.

JOHN. I ain't scared of Freddy Cole.

CALEB. Then why are you hiding from him?

(Instead of answering, JOHN *drinks.)*

CALEB. You fuck his woman? Piss on his boots?

JOHN. He's just a mean ol' redneck who got it out for me, is all. Had one since the day he met me.

*(*SIMON *re-enters with the cooked horse meat.)*

SIMON. Eat it if you're hungry, skip it if you ain't.

*(*JOHN *moves to his sack, pulls out knives and forks and then three dinner plates.)*

SIMON. Boy, you stole all that?

JOHN. No one else is going to be eating off it.

SIMON. That's Mrs. Taylor's fine china.

JOHN. That's Mrs. Taylor's *chipped* china. Which was laying on Mrs. Taylor's dirty floor. You want to eat with your hands? Be my guest. I'm using the utensils.

*(*SIMON *reluctantly reaches for them.* JOHN *hands them over.* SIMON *begins serving. As he does...)*

JOHN. Shabbat Shalom, Simon.

SIMON. Is it…Shabbat?

JOHN. It is. April 14, to be precise.

SIMON. Well, good Shabbat to you, then.

JOHN. Good Shabbat.

(**SIMON** *hands out the food.*)

JOHN. Never eaten horse before.

SIMON. Ain't nothing to it. Like any other meat. You hungry, right?

JOHN. Yeah.

SIMON. Well, then…

(**SIMON** *begins the blessing.* **JOHN** *joins in.* **CALEB** *does not.* **SIMON** *notices.*)

SIMON. *Barukh attah Adonai eloheinu melekh ha-olam, shehakol niheyah bidvaro.*

JOHN. Amen.

(**SIMON** *puts a piece of the meat in his mouth. They watch as he chews.*)

JOHN. Well?

SIMON. It's fine.

(**SIMON** *continues chewing. And chewing.*)

JOHN. You've been chewing that piece of meat longer than the horse was alive.

SIMON. It's chewy.

(**SIMON** *continues to chew.*)

SIMON. Very chewy.

(**SIMON** *finally – and with great difficulty – swallows.*)

SIMON. Well?

(**JOHN** *and* **CALEB** *cut into their meat and put a piece to their mouths. They eat in silence for a moment.*)

JOHN. It is chewy.

CALEB. Yes.

(All three eat in silence, intensely chewing. This lasts a while. Finally...)

SIMON. John, you say today is the fourteenth?

JOHN. It is.

SIMON. You know that puts us at Passover.

JOHN. Does it? I thought we might have missed it this year.

SIMON. Almost did. We're near the end now.

JOHN. Imagine that. Couldn't come at a better time.

CALEB. It comes every year at this time.

JOHN. You know what I'm talking about.

SIMON. I think he's talking about–

CALEB. I know what he means.

SIMON. –the fact that here we are this year, where we are this year, in the middle of all we are this year and Pesach happening at the same time.

JOHN. Why is this year different from all other years?

SIMON. It's a miracle, is what it is.

> I noticed, Caleb, that you weren't praying with us when we said the blessing. You forget your Hebrew?

CALEB. No.

SIMON. So, then...?

CALEB. I'm just not big on praying these days, Simon.

SIMON. Since when?

CALEB. Since Petersburg.

SIMON. Why?

CALEB. 'Cause I was at Petersburg...and He most decidedly was not.

SIMON. God is not fond of fair-weathered friends, Caleb.

CALEB. I don't need a sermon, Simon.

*(**JOHN** snickers.)*

JOHN. "Sermon, Simon."

SIMON. No, you don't need a sermon. And you ain't gonna get one. Not from me, at least. But when your mamma finds out you gave up praying...

CALEB. This sounds an awful lot like a sermon to me.

JOHN. It's a "simple Simon sermon."

SIMON. Course, we all pray in this house.

JOHN. That is true.

SIMON. And not just on the high holy days, neither, like some families I could mention.

JOHN. The Solomons, the Taylors, the Riveras!

SIMON. To mention just a few.

CALEB. Enough! I don't need a litany of all the under-observant Jews in Richmond. I stopped praying, I stopped believing. It's as simple as that.

SIMON. That is anything but simple. If you ask, He will provide.

CALEB. Oh, I asked. I did nothing but ask. For four years, I asked. At Petersburg, I asked. He was silent.

SIMON. War is not proof of God's absence. It's proof of His absence from men's hearts.

JOHN. Maybe God left Caleb before Caleb left God. Maybe that's why he fought this war.

CALEB. I fought to defend my home.

JOHN. From the look of things, I'd say you did a pretty lousy job of it.

CALEB. We were not going to be told how to live our lives.

JOHN. Oh. That must have rankled. Please tell us how that felt.

CALEB. You don't think I saw? You don't think I traveled around the last four years? I saw plantations. I saw... them out in the fields. I'm not blind to...to what this was.

JOHN. What? What was this? What's that word you keep choking on?

CALEB. I saw what...how people lived. I saw that this was not the noblest of...of–

JOHN. Of what? Peculiar institutions?

CALEB. I saw how field hands lived. And I saw how you lived. And I know there was a world of difference between the two. How did you spend the last four years, John?

Did you fight in this war? Did you break your back out
in a field? I don't need a lesson from you about what
this was. I know better than you do. I know what slavery was. I saw it. I know what war is. I lived it. What did
you see? What did you live? I was starving to death at
Petersburg and you were safe at home, reading novels.

(**JOHN** *takes the bottle away from* **CALEB** *and walks off
to the stairs and sits.*)

CALEB. Yes, reading, John. And you have my mother to
thank for that, don't forget.

JOHN. I taught myself how to read. Your mama taught
me "ABCDEFG" and by the time she got to "H," your
father had already put a stop to it.

CALEB. Because it was against the law.

JOHN. That's not why she stopped. She was so happy to
teach me to read. Mrs. DeLeon wanted me to be able
to read the Torah, which I did. Adam and Eve. Cain
and Abel. King Solomon. King David. And, of course,
Moses. The more I read, the more questions I asked.
Questions she didn't always have an answer for. Like,
when was God going to set us free like he did the slaves
in Egypt? Or whether Nat Turner was our new Moses.

SIMON. John, you need to settle down.

JOHN. You ever read Leviticus?
"Both thy bondman and thy bondmaids, which thou
shalt have, shall be of the heathen that are round about
you; of them shall ye buy bondmen and bondmaids.
They shall be your possession and ye shall take them
for your children to inherit for themselves.

JOHN. *(cont.)* They shall be your bondmen forever.
But over your brethren, the children of Israel, ye shall
not rule."
That's when she stopped teaching me to read. Because
I asked the simple yet obvious question: were we Jews
or were we slaves? Because, if Simon and I were Jews,
that seems to set your family's claims to faith directly
against ours, doesn't it?

CALEB. If you care to view the world in those kinds of absolutes.

JOHN. I was absolutely a slave. You were absolutely my master. You could absolutely discard all that you believe in. Because it was yours to discard if you wanted to. It was never ours. It was given to us and it could be taken away with just some careful reading of Leviticus.

SIMON. Is your faith that weak, John? Can't answer one question and it all falls apart?

JOHN. How do you square it, Simon?

SIMON. I can't. I can't square anything I don't understand. It ain't ours to square. That's why we always asking. Like you asked. Both of you asked your questions and sometimes you didn't get answers that you liked. But you kept on asking. That's what a Jew is. We talk with God, we wrestle with him. Sometimes we even argue with him. But we never stop asking, looking, hoping for answers. You don't lose your faith by not getting answers. You lose your faith by not asking questions at all. But you're still both asking. That gives me hope you ain't gone too far from believing what you know you wanna believe. This is who we are. This is our family.

JOHN. This is not my family!

SIMON. Only family you know.

JOHN. Not by choice.

SIMON. Who chooses their family? Whether you like it or not, we are a family.

JOHN. How?

SIMON. We shared a faith. And that faith came to us from Caleb's family. A gift. Generations brought up together in this house in the faith of God. That's a family.

JOHN. And how did that family treat us, Simon?

SIMON. Better than most.

JOHN. Not good enough.

SIMON. You know other slaves from round here. You know we had it a world better than they did. Coming here after your mamma died was the best thing that could have happened to you. You could have been sold to a plantation.

JOHN. You have no idea what went on in this house, Simon.

SIMON. Boy, don't you question me on the history of this house. I could write the history of this house. Could write your history, too.

JOHN. If you could write.

SIMON. Don't need to write to tell your story. You know your story?

JOHN. Better than you.

SIMON. You could put the things you know inside the things you don't and still have room for more. You were born in this house. Did you know that?

JOHN. I wasn't born in this house.

SIMON. You see? Already something he don't know and we just gettin' started. You was born here in this house and then you and your mama was sold to the Taylors next door. You was six when your mamma died. I get that right?

JOHN. Yeah.

SIMON. And back you came, sold back to the DeLeons. To have a mother in my Lizbeth. To be near young folks like Caleb and Sarah. You and Caleb were like two peas in a pod when you was little. Don't know what happened to that friendship.

CALEB. We were hardly that close.

JOHN. It wasn't a real friendship, Simon. Not when one friend tells the other what to do, pushes him around. Sends him off for whippings.

(pause)

SIMON. We ain't talking about whippings.

JOHN. Why not? We're talking about everything else. Why, if we were truly a family, did we get whipped like all the other slaves in town?

CALEB. Whipping was a rare and unfortunate occurrence.

JOHN. Unfortunate for who?

CALEB. Everyone.

JOHN. Simon and I got a couple of scars on our backs says it was a bit more unfortunate for us.

SIMON. I don't need you to speak for me.

CALEB. Simon was never whipped.

SIMON. I don't need you to speak for me, neither.

CALEB. My father only had his slaves whipped when it was absolutely necessary. Perhaps, John, you have so many scars on your back because you needed to be disciplined more than others.

(pause)

JOHN. Lizbeth used to say to Sarah and me: "you listen to Mr. DeLeon. You do as you told. Or they gonna send you to the Whipping Man. The Whipping Man gonna take all the skin off your back." He was like the devil, the Whipping Man. Smelled of whiskey, sweat and shit, like he hadn't bathed in years. Probably hadn't. He'd pick up the slaves and put them in chains and take them to his shop. There were blood stains on the walls. And a large collection of bullwhips, too. He used them depending on his mood. First time I was sent there, he used a pearl handled bullwhip.
Didn't he, Caleb?

SIMON. How would Caleb know?

CALEB. John, I…

JOHN. Because Caleb went with me the first time I was sent. Didn't you, Caleb?

(silence)

JOHN. Mr. DeLeon wanted him to learn the true relationship between a master and his slave.
What happened first, Caleb? You remember?

(No answer from CALEB.)

JOHN. The Whipping Man put me on my knees, didn't he?

He took off my shirt. He attached my hands to two leather straps. And I was whipped.

(On "whipped," JOHN stomps the floor with his foot then claps his hands together. The sound he makes is a rhythmic "boom-smack.")

JOHN. And whipped.

(Boom-smack!)

And whipped.

(Boom-smack!)

And whipped.

(Boom-smack!)

Wasn't I, Caleb?

(Again, no answer.)

JOHN. Then in the middle of the whipping, I heard Caleb's voice.

"Stop!" he yelled. "Stop!"

I thought to myself, "Caleb is saving me. Caleb is rescuing me. Caleb cares about me."

And then I heard Caleb say, "I want to do it myself."

The Whipping Man handed Caleb the bullwhip. And Caleb whipped me. Didn't you, Caleb? You whipped me.

(Boom-SMACK!)

And whipped me.

(Boom-SMACK!)

JOHN. *(cont.)* And whipped me.

(Boom-SMACK!)

(Boom-SMACK!)

(Boom-SMACK!)

(JOHN walks to CALEB and crouches down in his face. They stare at one another for a moment.)

That's when we stopped being as close as you remember, Simon.

(**JOHN** *grabs the bottle and exits to the kitchen.*)

(**CALEB** *and* **SIMON** *sit in silence a moment.*)

CALEB. What John said…what I did…

SIMON. You did what you did. We all did what we did. They ain't no reason to go into it no more. John wants to fight with the world. I just want my family back.

CALEB. John says my father promised you money when he returns.

SIMON. He did, at that.

CALEB. Well, that's good.

SIMON. It is a good thing, yes.

CALEB. What will you do?

SIMON. We gonna build a house.

CALEB. A house, really? That's nice.

SIMON. Very nice, yes. Gonna have me a house and a family to come home to at the end of the day. Own something. Be something.

CALEB. John says he's going to New York with the money my father promised him.

SIMON. New York? Shoot, that's news to me. I'll believe that when I see it. John talks big, but John acts small.

CALEB. Says he's been planning it ever since my father told him about the money.

SIMON. Your father? He never told John nothing. I told John this morning about the money. Any plans he been making ain't more than a day old.

CALEB. Why would he lie?

SIMON. He is John.

CALEB. What are your plans after you build your house?

SIMON. Your father said I could work here, still. For wages. Sarah and Lizbeth, too.

CALEB. You'd stay here?

SIMON. Ya'll still gonna need a cook, a maid, a…well, a Simon. Who else knows this house better than me?

CALEB. No one.

SIMON. Shoot, ya'll can't afford to do without me. God knows you can't. Nah, this is the one thing I was always good at. And I'm gonna keep being good at it. 'Cept this time for money.

A lot of money.

CALEB. It's good that you're staying. It'll be like before.

(pause)

SIMON. No. No, it will not be like before.

CALEB. Did you hate us, Simon?

SIMON. No.

CALEB. Were you happy?

SIMON. Wasn't my place to be happy.

(pause)

SIMON. Now, I know we ain't got all that much round here, despite what John's been bringin' in, but I am going to try and have a Seder tomorrow.

CALEB. A Seder?

SIMON. I was thinking God would forgive us if we're a little late this year, seeing as they's special circumstances and all.

CALEB. Simon, I can't. I just…can't anymore.

SIMON. Then don't. I'm not asking your permission. I'm telling you I'm going to have a Seder. I ain't missed a Seder in all my years. I'll be damned if I miss it this year.

CALEB. You had a Seder every year?

SIMON. What kind of Jews would we be if we didn't have ourselves a Seder every year?

CALEB. I just thought…

SIMON. We had ours back there in the kitchen when you was having yours. You never knew that?

CALEB. Never. You know the ceremony?

SIMON. I remember it pretty well, yes.

CALEB. We'll send John out to steal a Haggadah.

SIMON. Already got me a Haggadah. Gift from your grand-daddy, years ago.

CALEB. Can you read it?

SIMON. Not a word. But I have it.

CALEB. But you don't have anything for the ceremony.

SIMON. I've been thinking about that.

CALEB. You need an egg.

SIMON. Got one or two left from the lot John stole this morning.

CALEB. Stolen eggs for your Seder. Perfect. What else? A shank bone.

SIMON. Well, we ain't yet had the time to bury yours.

(He gestures to **CALEB***'s leg.)*

CALEB. You're joking.

SIMON. I'm just looking for ideas.

CALEB. Well, look elsewhere.

SIMON. I got the bones from this old horse. I can use those.

CALEB. What about bitter herbs?

SIMON. There's some collard greens still growing out in the garden.

CALEB. They're bitter?

SIMON. Raw? Very bitter. That's why most folks cook 'em up in hog fat. We won't be doing that for the Seder, of course.

CALEB. You're not going to find any wine around here.

SIMON. John's whiskey'll have to do.

CALEB. Isn't whiskey forbidden right now?

SIMON. None of this is exactly kosher.

CALEB. Oh, but the matzo…

SIMON. I already thought of that. You know that hard, cracker stuff the soldiers used to carry with them? Made of flour and water and not much else?

CALEB. Hardtack?

SIMON. That's what it's called! Hardtack, yes!

CALEB. Soldiers have been choking down hardtack for four years, you want to serve it at a Seder?

SIMON. It's about as unleavened as you can get.

CALEB. Yeah, but where are we going to find hardtack at…?

*(**SIMON** reaches his pocket to remove a handkerchief wrapped around three pieces of hardtack.)*

CALEB. Where'd you get that?

SIMON. The hospital. Union fella gave it to me before I left.

CALEB. You could have eaten that.

SIMON. I could have, yes. But then what would we have used for our Seder? No, this hardtack is special. We'll eat it tomorrow.

CALEB. You will.

SIMON. We will.

CALEB. We might.

*(A moment, then **SIMON** begins gathering up the dishes and silverware. As he does, **JOHN** re-enters, drunker than before.)*

JOHN. That's good, there, Simon. Clean all that up.

*(**SIMON** exits in silence.)*

JOHN. So we're having a Seder tomorrow?

CALEB. Seems that way.

JOHN. That seems right. That seems right and good that we do. Let's celebrate the freeing of the slaves. Out of Egypt. Out of Richmond.
Maybe I'll become a rabbi.

CALEB. That's a sensible idea.

JOHN. You think?

CALEB. You'll have quite a congregation. All the Jewish Negroes in Virginia.

JOHN. I think there'd be enough for a minyan.
I could go to college. Up North. I could go to Harvard.

CALEB. You couldn't get in to Harvard.

JOHN. Then I probably shouldn't go.

   Maybe I'll write a book like Frederick Douglass.

CALEB. Maybe you will.

JOHN. And maybe I'll even put you in it: Caleb Legree.

CALEB. You're enjoying this, aren't you?

JOHN. What?

CALEB. Settling scores.

JOHN. Is that what I'm doing?

CALEB. I don't know what you're doing. Why are you here?

JOHN. I'm waiting for my money.

CALEB. The money my father told you he'd give you?

JOHN. That's right.

CALEB. Simon just told me that my father never said that
   to you.

JOHN. Did he?

CALEB. You only found out today when Simon told you.

JOHN. So?

CALEB. So you lied to me.

JOHN. So what if I did? I'm still here waiting for it, aren't I?

CALEB. But why did you come back here in the first place?
   I know why you're staying. I just don't understand why
   you came back.

JOHN. I live here.

CALEB. No, you don't. Not anymore. You're free, remember?

JOHN. This is the only home I've ever known.

CALEB. The home you hated. Why are you here, John? It
   wasn't for the money and it certainly wasn't to remi-
   nisce.

JOHN. Where are all the other Confederate soldiers?

CALEB. I don't know what you're–

JOHN. Why are you here and no one else is? Why are you
   sneaking home in the middle of the night, riding a
   dead horse and there are no other Rebs in sight?

CALEB. Why's Freddy Cole lookin' for you? Did he do that to your hand?

JOHN. No. I cut it.

CALEB. On what?

JOHN. Piece of glass.

CALEB. Breaking into a home?

JOHN. Maybe.

CALEB. Maybe you should have Simon look at it.

JOHN. Maybe you should worry about your own wounds.

CALEB. Maybe the people who you robbed would want to know what you've been up to.

JOHN. If you could find them.

CALEB. They'll be back eventually.

JOHN. Maybe I'll be gone by then.

CALEB. Maybe my father would like to know what you've been up to.

JOHN. Maybe you'd like to know what he's been up to.

CALEB. You know something you're not telling me?

JOHN. Where's your pardon?

CALEB. My–

JOHN. Your pardon. Officers and soldiers at Appomattox were pardoned. If you were there like you said, you'd have a pardon. Piece of paper. Something.

CALEB. I–

JOHN. Where is it?

CALEB. It's hidden.

JOHN. Where?

CALEB. I'm not telling you.

JOHN. Show it to me.

CALEB. No.

JOHN. Why not?

CALEB. 'Cause it's mine.

JOHN. You know what I think?

CALEB. I don't care what you think.

JOHN. I think you weren't anywhere near Appomattox. I think you surrendered long before the rest of your army did. I think you're a deserter.

CALEB. You can think whatever you want.

JOHN. I bet I can prove it, too. It's why you didn't want to go to the hospital, isn't it? You go there, someone's gonna figure out your story. So you have your surgery here. Have Simon care for your wounds, get you food. Oh and, of course, hide you if anyone comes looking for you. That about sum it up?

CALEB. You certainly are the expert on asking Simon to hide you from people who are looking for you. Aren't you, John?

(No answer from **JOHN.***)*

CALEB. And even if what you're saying were true, what difference does it make now? The war is over and–

JOHN. And your side lost and you weren't there when it happened. What about the men you abandoned, the men you were responsible for leading, Captain DeLeon? Deserting the army is one thing, but you deserted your men. They'll hang you from the nearest branch the second they find you.

CALEB. I'm home now. Even if they come here, Simon wouldn't give me up.

JOHN. What if Simon wasn't here?

CALEB. Where would he go?

JOHN. Let's say he goes out looking for his family?

CALEB. Why would he do that? They're with my father.

*(***JOHN*** slowly shakes his head "no.")*

CALEB. What? Tell me, goddamnit!

JOHN. They're gone.

CALEB. They're with my father.

JOHN. No they are not. They. Are. Gone.

CALEB. Gone where?

JOHN. Just gone. Sold. Your father waited until your mother was gone, until Simon was gone and then he sold them.

CALEB. Why would he do that?

JOHN. You can't think of a reason? Caleb? Why your father might not want Sarah in the house anymore?

CALEB. I don't know what you're talking about.

JOHN. Caleb.

(long, confessional pause)

CALEB. Why now?

JOHN. When was your last leave? Before you were sent back to Petersburg?

CALEB. I don't remember.

JOHN. September.
Seven months ago.
Things have started to become quite...apparent in that time.

(pause)

CALEB. Sarah is...?

JOHN. Sarah is.

CALEB. You've known all this time and not said anything to me?

JOHN. What do I owe you?

CALEB. What do you owe Simon?

JOHN. If I had told Simon the second I saw him, what do you think would have happened to you? Think he would have stayed around and helped you with your leg?

CALEB. Of course he would have.

JOHN. Why?

CALEB. Because he wouldn't have left me like that.

JOHN. You're sure about that? Why don't we go ahead and tell Simon now and see what he does?

CALEB. Why don't we?
Simon! Simon, get in here!

JOHN. And then say he leaves. And you're here, alone and helpless.

CALEB. Well, you–

JOHN. Well I what?

CALEB. You would leave me like this?

JOHN. I would leave you much worse.

CALEB. They are out there, John. Simon needs to find them.

JOHN. Then let him go find them. I'll gladly take you to the hospital. Why don't we just grab your pardon and go?

CALEB. You know we can't.

JOHN. Yes I do.

CALEB. What are we going to do?

JOHN. We're not going to do anything, we're not going to say anything.

CALEB. But Sarah–

JOHN. If you tell Simon, he will leave. And when Simon leaves, I leave. That I promise. And then you're on your own.

CALEB. So what, then?

JOHN. We wait like we have been. We let your father tell Simon when he gets home. If he gets home.

CALEB. They'll be long gone by then.

JOHN. They're long gone already.

*(**SIMON** enters.)*

SIMON. Caleb? You wanted something?

(pause)

CALEB. Nothing, Simon. I'm sorry.

End of Scene Three

Scene Four

(The next evening. Saturday, April 15, 1865.)

(The rain continues.)

(The room is now filled with even more possessions from the neighboring homes: a chandelier, rolls of carpets, paintings and furniture and stacks of silverware. The book collection has grown considerably. There are also more candles about, some in lamps, others bare.)

(In the middle of the room, all the makings of a Seder are set about on the floor as if on a table.)

(The lights rise on **CALEB**, *sleeping.* **JOHN** *enters with some of the necessities for the Seder. He has been setting the table.)*

(He goes to the window and furtively looks out, then goes back to his work. He is a bundle of nervous energy.)

(He comes to a stopping place in the work and grabs a book and sits down to read.)

*(**CALEB** wakes up.)*

CALEB. I'm thirsty.

JOHN. Simon'll be back soon.

(pause)

CALEB. Can you please get me some water?

JOHN. I'm reading.

CALEB. John…

*(**JOHN** ignores him.)*

CALEB. What are you reading?

JOHN. Dickens.

CALEB. Which?

JOHN. "Great Expectations."

CALEB. Can you hand me a book?

*(**JOHN** ignores him.)*

CALEB. Can you please hand me a book so that I might stop pestering you and let you read in peace?

(JOHN reaches for a book and without checking to see what it is, tosses it to CALEB, who opens it to the title page.)

CALEB. "Richmond Municipal Code, Revised 1847." Thank you, John.

(He waits for JOHN to send him another book. Once it's clear he's not going to, CALEB resigns himself to reading the one he has.)

(They read in silence a moment.)

(There is some movement on the front porch. JOHN and CALEB both tense up at this, waiting for who it might be. The door opens: it is SIMON. He slowly enters, as if all his energy were gone.)

JOHN. Where've you been, Simon? You were gone a long time.

SIMON. I went to the market.

CALEB. Simon, I'm thirsty.

(SIMON sits.)

CALEB. John wouldn't give me any water.

SIMON. I'll get some water soon enough, Caleb.

JOHN. I set up for the Seder, like you asked.

SIMON. I see that, thank you.

JOHN. Sun's going down. We should probably start soon.

(pause)

SIMON. The President's dead.

JOHN. What?

SIMON. He's dead.

JOHN. How?

SIMON. Shot. Last night. In Washington. At a theatre. He's gone.

(silence)

SIMON. I wouldn't have believed it if I didn't hear it with my own ears. Right there in the middle of the market, fella rides up and just says it. Announces it like he's callin' a dance. Folks started cheering and whooping. Dancin'. Town started going crazy. Crazier than it's been last few weeks, even. All them folks was so happy. The white folks, anyway.

(silence)

(**JOHN** *looks at* **CALEB**, *who is stifling a laugh.*)

JOHN. You think this is funny, Caleb?

CALEB. As a matter of fact, I do. That dumb son of a bitch gets through the entire war and gets shot while watching a play? Fitting. They say who shot him?

SIMON. Some actor. Um, Booth, I think they said?

(**CALEB** *stops laughing.*)

CALEB. Edwin?

SIMON. I don't know.

CALEB. John Wilkes?

SIMON. Maybe him.

CALEB. My God. I saw him play Hamlet here in Richmond a few years ago. He's been to this house before.

JOHN. I remember him. Slippery fella. Figures he's a friend of the family.

SIMON. The Federals are all over the place now. More comin' in all the time. They think he come to Richmond. They're blockin' the roads, the bridges, all the ins and outs. No one's going nowhere 'til they find him.

Father Abraham. I met him. I tell you that?

JOHN. You met Abraham Lincoln?

SIMON. Just the other day, when he came into Richmond.

CALEB. Lincoln was here?

SIMON. Walked out in the middle of the town. He was a sight to see. Just as tall as they said. Taller. He wore a hat that stretched up to the sky. Made him all that much taller. But when he walked, his shoulders was rounded and he slouched a bit, like he was scared of being up so high. It didn't matter, though. That man had height to spare. He looked to be two hundred years old. His eyes were sunk down in his face and his wrinkles was deeper than any I've ever seen on a man. Like someone took a knife and carved them in. He had a whole crowd of folks around him. Colored folks. They followed him and touched him and kissed his hands. No one had to tell me who he was. Even if I hadn't seen his picture before, I still woulda known. Proudest day of my life. He was coming towards where I was standing. I walked to him. And I stopped right in front of him. And he stopped. And we looked at each other.

JOHN. What'd you do?

SIMON. I bowed.

JOHN. You bowed?

SIMON. Only thing I could think to do.

JOHN. What did he do?

SIMON. He bowed back. Only thing he could think to do, I guess.
That was a great man. Father Abraham.

JOHN. There are no great men anymore.

SIMON. Lincoln was one.

JOHN. He was a politician.

CALEB. He was a tyrant.

SIMON. He was a savior. Father Abraham set us free. There's your Moses, John.

JOHN. Abraham Lincoln was not Moses. He didn't lead us anywhere. He just opened the door and looked the other way. He wasn't a savior. He was just a man, doing what needed to be done to "save the country."

CALEB. What country? What did he save? What's left to claim? Look at where we are. Look at what we have. You might not have liked what came before but it was a hell of a lot better than what we got now. Abraham Lincoln didn't make free men out of you. He made slaves of us all. In that, we are all truly equal.

SIMON. Caleb, I need you to stop talking right now.

JOHN. Tell him, Simon.

SIMON. You too, John.

JOHN. Me? I…

SIMON. You two been arguing since you both got back. And you're gonna keep arguing til you're old and grey. But you ain't gonna be doing it tonight. I ain't got a lot. I got my God and my family. And until tonight, I had the man who set me free. And now he's gone. And my family ain't with me. So all I have is my God and this day and what we're about to do. You understand? So now that you've said your peace, you gonna leave me in peace to do this Seder. I don't wanna hear nothing from either of you that wasn't originally said in Hebrew, you understand me?

JOHN. Yeah, Simon.

SIMON. Caleb?

CALEB. I'm sorry, Simon.

Simon, there's…

JOHN. Simon, I think we should get started on our Seder. It'll be good for us, don't you think?

SIMON. Yes. Yes, it will.

JOHN. Take our minds off our troubles and give it up to God.

SIMON. That's right. That is right. Good, then. I've got a few more things I need to get from the kitchen, then we'll be ready to start.

(SIMON exits.)

CALEB. We have to tell him.

JOHN. We don't have to do a thing, you understand me?

CALEB. He thinks his family's coming back.

JOHN. Let him enjoy his Seder.

CALEB. You don't care about him.

JOHN. And you do? Go on and tell him, then. Open his eyes. Then open your own. Did you even hear what he said? The town is crawling with Federal soldiers now, 'cause of Lincoln. You want to be brought to them without a pardon in your hand? Road block in and out of town? Nowhere to go, Caleb. You best make do with what you got here.

(SIMON *re-enters with a Haggadah and a bottle of whiskey.*)

SIMON. *(handing* JOHN *the Haggadah)* Take this, John. Read along in case I forget. I'm gonna be jumping around a bit. Just make sure I stay on the tracks.
Caleb?

CALEB. Yeah?

SIMON. You gonna do this with us?

CALEB. If you'll let me.

SIMON. All are welcome. Good, good.

(SIMON *goes to the door and cracks it open for Elijah. He then moves to the place setting and sits.* SIMON *takes the bottle of whiskey and pours a small amount into one of the glasses.* JOHN *joins them, lighting the candles at the table setting.*)

SIMON. All right, then.

(SIMON *holds up one of the glasses.*)

SIMON. Behold this cup of...

(He chuckles.)

...wine. Let it be a symbol of our joy tonight as we celebrate the festival of Pesach.

(He sets the whiskey down.)

SIMON. Praised be you, O Lord our God, King of the Universe, who creates the fruit of the vine and who has sanctified us by your commandments.

JOHN. Well done, Simon.

SIMON. Not bad for an old man, huh?

JOHN. Not bad at all.

SIMON. I have no idea what comes next.

JOHN. "As a token of thy love…"

SIMON. Yes! As a token of thy love, O Lord our God, you have given us occasions for rejoicing, festivals and holidays for happiness, this Feast of Unleavened Bread, the season of our liberation from bondage in Egypt. You have…um…

JOHN. "…quickened."

SIMON. I'm going as fast as I can.

JOHN. That's the word, "quickened." "Quickened within us the desire to serve–"

SIMON. Ah, yes, the desire to serve you, and in joy and gladness, has bestowed on us your holy festivals. Praised be you, O Lord our God, King of the universe, who has kept us in life, and sustained us, and enabled us to reach this season.

If only by the skin of our teeth.

JOHN. Amen.

SIMON. That's right.

(They sit there a moment, waiting for **SIMON** *to drink.)*

JOHN. You're supposed to drink, Simon.

SIMON. I know.

CALEB. Do you drink?

SIMON. Not a drop in all my life.

*(***JOHN*** reaches for it but* **SIMON** *bats his hand away and takes the glass, himself. He looks at it and brings it to his lips. He lets the whiskey slide down this throat. It tastes like freedom. He closes his eyes.)*

SIMON. *(sings)*

When Israel was in Egypt's Land,

Let my people go!

Oppressed so hard they could not stand,

Let my people go!

Go down, Moses,

Way down in Egypt's Land.

Tell ol' Pharaoh,

Let my people go!

(SIMON takes the collard greens off the plate and hands them to JOHN and CALEB, keeping one for himself.)

SIMON. Blessed art thou, O Lord our God, King of the Universe who created the fruit of the Earth.

(They dip the greens in the salt water and eat them.)

SIMON. Caleb, break the hardtack now and read some.

(CALEB picks up the hardtack and breaks it in two. JOHN hands him the Haggadah. As CALEB reads, SIMON leans back, great satisfaction on his face. He continues to hum the verse of "Go Down, Moses.")

CALEB. "Behold the mazzah, symbol of the Bread of Poverty our ancestors–"

SIMON. Whose ancestors?

CALEB. Our ancestors.

SIMON. Yes, sir.

CALEB. "–our ancestors were made to eat in their affliction, when they were slaves in the land of Egypt. Let it remind us of our fellow men who are today poor and hungry."

SIMON. Would that they could come and eat with us! Read, John.

(JOHN takes the Haggadah from CALEB. SIMON continues to hum "Go Down Moses.")

JOHN. "We have dedicated this festival tonight to the dream and the hope of freedom. The dream and the hope that have filled the hearts of men from the time our Israelite ancestors went forth out of Egypt."

SIMON. *(sings)*

Tell old Pharaoh,

Let my people go!

(speaks)

People have suffered, nations have struggled to make this dream come true.

JOHN. That's right.

SIMON. Yes, sir. Now we dedicate ourselves to the struggle for freedom. Though the sacrifice be great and the hardships many, we shall not rest until the chains that enslave all men be broken.

CALEB. Broken…

SIMON. *(triumphant singing)*

Let my people go!

(spoken)

But the freedom we strive for means more than broken chains. What does it mean, John? Read.

JOHN. "It means liberation from all those enslavements that warp the spirit and blight the mind…"

SIMON. That's right.

JOHN. "…that destroy the soul even though they leave the flesh alive."

SIMON. For men can be enslaved in more ways than one. Name one, John.

JOHN. "Men can be enslaved to themselves."

SIMON. How?

JOHN. "When they let emotion sway them to their hurt, when they permit harmful habits to tyrannize over them – they are slaves."

SIMON. You with your drinking, for example.

How else, Caleb? Read.

(CALEB takes the Haggadah.)

CALEB. "When laziness or cowardice keeps them from doing…"

(He stops.)

SIMON. It won't bite you. Read!

CALEB. "When laziness or cowardice keeps them from doing what they know to be right – they are slaves."

SIMON. They are slaves. John…

(JOHN takes the book, reads.)

JOHN. "When the work men do enriches others, but leaves them in want of strong houses for shelter, they are slaves."

SIMON. They are slaves!
     Caleb?

CALEB. They are slaves.

SIMON. Read.

CALEB. "How deeply those enslavements have scarred the world!"

SIMON. Oh, how painful!

CALEB. "The wars!"

SIMON. Mmmm.

CALEB. "The destruction!"

SIMON. Mmmm!

CALEB. "The suffering!"

SIMON & JOHN. Mmmm!

CALEB. "The waste!"

SIMON & JOHN. Mmmm!

CALEB. *(more to himself)* My God, the waste…

SIMON. Pesach calls us to be what?

JOHN. Free!

SIMON. From the tyranny of our own selves!

JOHN. Free!

SIMON. From the enslavement of poverty and inequality!

JOHN & CALEB. Free!

SIMON. From the corroding hate that eats away the ties which unite mankind!

JOHN & CALEB. Free!

SIMON. Pesach calls upon us to put and end to all slavery!

JOHN That's right.

SIMON. To all slavery! Pesach cried out in the name of God
     (sings)
     LET MY PEOPLE GO!

CALEB. *(reading)* "Pesach summons us to freedom."

SIMON. Freedom.

CALEB. Freedom.

SIMON. Let freedom ring in this house!

JOHN. Yes, sir.

SIMON. Let freedom ring in this city!

JOHN. Mmmhmm.

SIMON. Let freedom ring in this nation!

JOHN. That's right.

SIMON. Sing it with me.

> *(singing)*
> Go down, Moses!
> Way back in Egypt's Land.

SIMON & JOHN. *(singing)*
> Tell ol' Pharaoh,
> Let my people go.

SIMON. Why is this night different from all other nights?

CALEB. You can't ask the questions, Simon, that's my job.

JOHN. I'm the youngest. I should ask.

SIMON. I'll ask. I wanna see if you have any answers for me. A child has questions. A man has answers.

On all other nights we eat either leavened or unleavened bread; why on this night are we eating this hardtack? Caleb?

CALEB. Because our forefathers left Egypt in such a hurry, there was no time for the dough to bake properly. It baked flat, in the sun. The first Seder was improvised, like ours.

SIMON. Imagine that.

John, on all other nights we eat all kinds of herbs. Why, on this night, do we eat only bitter herbs?

JOHN. To remind us of the bitterness of slavery. As if we needed reminding.

SIMON. Your children will. And their children will. We will never forget. We must not forget. Your children must be taught. Yours too, Caleb.

(Let this sink in.)

SIMON. On all other nights we do not think of dipping our

food in water or in anything else; why, on this night, are we dipping these greens in salt water?

CALEB. To remind us of the tears of slavery.

SIMON. Tears that we will cry no more!

CALEB. Simon…

SIMON. And if we had any Haroseth?

JOHN. To remind us that sweetness can come from bitterness.

SIMON. The sweet fruit of freedom!

On all other nights we eat sitting up at the table; why, on this night, do we recline?

CALEB. Simon…

JOHN. Because reclining, because rest, is the symbol of the free man.

SIMON. Read, Caleb.

*(**CALEB** hesitates, the takes up the book again.)*

CALEB. "Once we were slaves to Pharaoh in Egypt, but the Lord, our God, brought us forth with a strong hand and an outstretched arm. If God had not brought our forefathers out of Egypt, we and our children and our children's children might still be enslaved…"

(He hesitates.)

SIMON. Go on.

JOHN. Caleb.

*(**CALEB** is silent a moment longer.)*

CALEB. He sold them.

SIMON. What?

CALEB. He sold them.

SIMON. Sold? Who?

CALEB. Sarah and Elizabeth.

(An eternity.)

SIMON. No.

CALEB. It's true.

SIMON. No.

CALEB. I'm sorry.

SIMON. NO!!!

*(**SIMON** stands up, grabs the whiskey bottle and throws it at the front door. It shatters.)*

SIMON. Why?
WHY!!!

CALEB. She was…

SIMON. WHY?!?

CALEB. She was expecting.

*(He gets in **CALEB**'s face.)*

SIMON. Where'd they go?

CALEB. I don't know.

SIMON. WHERE'D THEY GO?!?

CALEB. I don't know!

SIMON. Who bought them?

(silence)

SIMON. WHO BOUGHT THEM!!

*(**SIMON** grabs him by the shirt.)*

SIMON. You think I'm playin' around?

CALEB. John? Tell him.

SIMON. John, you knew about this? You knew about this?

*(**SIMON** grabs **JOHN** and pins him against the wall, shaking him as he speaks.)*

SIMON. Three days. Three days you knew they was sold and you said NOTHING?

JOHN. Simon, I–

SIMON. You said NOTHING to me. Three days I coulda been out looking for my family. You said NOTHING.

JOHN. Simon–

SIMON. Where'd they go?

JOHN. I don't know.

SIMON. Who has them?

JOHN. I don't know!

SIMON. Why you keep it from me?

JOHN. Simon, I–

SIMON. WHY?

JOHN. I needed to hide.

SIMON. From Freddy Cole.

JOHN. From Freddy Cole.

SIMON. Why?

JOHN. Just because.

SIMON. Just because of why, John?

    (shakes him hard)

    WHY?

JOHN. *(terrified)* I…I…I killed, I killed someone.
    FreddyFreddy saw.

SIMON. Who did you kill?
    WHO?

JOHN. The Whipping Man.

SIMON. John…

JOHN. It was an accident.

SIMON. You don't accidentally kill the Whipping Man.
    What happened?

    (No answer. Simon shakes him.)

SIMON. WHAT HAPPENED?

JOHN. It was in his shop the day Richmond fell. Mr.
    DeLeon sold Elizabeth and Sarah and I tried to stop
    him. He sent me to the Whipping Man andandand
    in the middle of the whipping, thestrapthestrap, the
    leather strap–

SIMON. *(shakes him)* What about it?

JOHN. It snapped during the whipping. It was old, brittle.
    It just snapped, snapped off. And I grabbed the whip
    from him, as it was coming to me. And I took it from
    him. I don't know why I did it.

SIMON. And?

JOHN. And I whipped him.

SIMON. John…

JOHN. Just like he whipped me.

SIMON. John…

JOHN. He was on the ground. And I took the handle – the pearl handle he used on me – and I beat him with it.

SIMON. John…

JOHN. I beat him and beat him and beat him.

And I killed him.

I killed him, Simon.

SIMON. John, John, John…you are a dead man, you know that.

JOHN. Am I?

SIMON. You killed a white man. You killed The Whipping Man. In this town? Now? You're lost, John. You are lost.

JOHN. Simon, I'm scared. Please, Simon…

SIMON. All this time…

JOHN. I'm sorry.

(SIMON *finally lets him go and walks away.*)

CALEB. That's why you didn't tell him…

JOHN. Simon, I'm sorry.

CALEB. …it's because you can't leave, can you?

JOHN. I don't want to hear a word from you.

CALEB. Freddy's after you. And if he sees you, he'll kill you. And now that the roads are blocked, you're trapped here. You can't leave this town.

(*to* SIMON)

He didn't tell you because he knew that once you found out, you'd go looking for them. He kept this from you so he could stay safe. He needed you, he lied to you and he used you.

JOHN. And what have you been doing all this time, Caleb?

(*to* SIMON)

Caleb, here…reason he's so afraid to go to the hospital? He's a deserter.

CALEB. Simon, I–

SIMON. I don't need no explanations from you. Two lying, deceitful peas in a pod.

JOHN. I was scared, Simon. I had no choice.

SIMON. No. You're free now. For the first time in your life, you do have a choice. You had a choice and you made a choice. When you was beating that man to death, you made a choice. When you hid from Freddy Cole, you made a choice. When you lied to me about my family, you made a choice. I see the choices you made. They tell me all I need to know about the man you are, about the free man you gonna be. You don't get to be free, you work to be free. It's what we been praying for tonight. What you should have learned from all your reading. Were we Jews or were we slaves? I know what you were. You ain't no Jew. You ain't even a man. You just a nigger, John. Nigger, Nigger, Nigger John.

CALEB. Simon, I'm so sorry.

SIMON. What good your sorries gonna do me? Your sorries gonna bring back my family?

CALEB. No.

SIMON. Then keep them. I don't need them.

You think I didn't know, Caleb, what you was doing with my daughter?

CALEB. Simon, you know me. You know my family. You know that's not how it was.

SIMON. I been around houses in town. I seen what happens to slave girls there. I know how it was.

CALEB. I loved her.

SIMON. YOU OWNED HER!

You loved her? How did you love her, Caleb? Like a dog. You love a dog, you feed a dog. But when he acts up, you also beat a dog. You might have thought you loved Sarah but you also owned her. And if this hadn't all just happened, you would have owned your baby, too. You would have owned your own child, Caleb.

CALEB. No, that's not how it was.

SIMON. You don't know how it was. You don't know what this was. You don't have any idea. This is what this was.

(SIMON takes off his shirt to reveal a horrible patchwork of scars on his back from various whippings through his life.)

SIMON. You see this? From the Whipping Man. From your father, too. And from your grandfather. I got your family tree right here on my back. You see? Your wounds are gonna heal. You gonna rebuild your city. You gonna rejoin your nation. You gonna be a citizen. What are we gonna be? What are we gonna have? We gonna have these. You gonna go on with your life and forget you ever had a family of slaves living in your house. Forget all about us. But we always gonna remember. We gonna have the proof of it every time we look at ourselves, at our skin, on our backs. Our skin gonna remind us for the rest of our lives and our children's lives. And now your children's lives, too, Caleb. This is your legacy. This is your family's legacy.

(SIMON grabs his hat and coat, a rucksack and his rifle.)

SIMON. I'm leaving. I'm going off to find my family. My wife. My daughter. My grandchild. I lost too much time. God only knows where they might be.

CALEB. It's dark, Simon.

SIMON. Yes, it is. But I will be going.

CALEB. The roadblocks.

SIMON. Let them try and stop me.

(SIMON starts to exit. JOHN grabs him by the arm.)

JOHN. Simon, wait.

SIMON. What?

JOHN. Take me with you.

SIMON. Take yourself.

JOHN. I can't leave. I can't go out there.

SIMON. How is that my problem?

JOHN. Freddy's after me.

SIMON. You got to solve this on your own, boy.

JOHN. I can't stay here.

SIMON. Then leave.

JOHN. I can't leave.

SIMON. Then stay.

JOHN. I can't! Simon, please! I don't know where to go. I don't know what to do.

SIMON. You're free now.

JOHN. BUT WHAT AM I SUPPOSED TO DO????

*(**SIMON** stops and looks at both of them.)*

SIMON. Looks like you two need each other. Both of you need help from each other.

JOHN. I won't help him.

SIMON. Well, that is your choice, ain't it? Help him, don't help him. Stay here, don't stay. Ain't my problem no more. Two peas in a pod.

*(**SIMON** takes his Haggadah.)*

SIMON. I wouldn't feel too badly if I were you, Caleb. You ain't the only man in your family to have a baby with a slave. It's time you knew that fact. Things don't change that much from father to son. That much I can see.
Or, I guess, from brother to brother.
That much I can see now, too.

*(**SIMON** slowly begins exiting.)*

SIMON. When the Lord will return the exiles of Zion, we will have been like dreamers.

JOHN. Simon…

SIMON. Then our mouths will be filled with laughter, and our tongues with joyous song.

JOHN. Simon, please!

SIMON. Then will they say among the nations, "The Lord has done great things for us."

CALEB. Simon…

SIMON. Next year in Jerusalem! Next year in Freedom!

(**SIMON** *exits.*)

(**JOHN** *walks to the open door and stands there, watching* **SIMON** *leave. The world stands there before him through that open door. He cannot move through it, though.*)

(**JOHN** *slams the door and walks back into the house. He grabs the bottle, sits down on the floor and takes a drink. After a long moment, he offers the bottle to* **CALEB.** **CALEB** *takes the bottle and drinks, then hands the bottle back to* **JOHN.**)

(*They pass the bottle between themselves.*)

(*The rain continues.*)

(*The lights slowly fade on them.*)

The End

PROP LIST

Hand Props
Shotgun
Lantern
Handkerchief
Pocket knife
John's rucksack, filled with:
• Whiskey bottle #2
Whiskey bottle #3
Wooden toolbox with saw
Bucket
Bloody Rags
Scrub Brush
Cup of hot water
Sacks of pilfered goods #2 & #3
Small sack of coffee
Handful of eggs
Whiskey bottle #4
Two burlap sacks (#5 and #6)
Utensils and metal items
Whiskey bottle #5
Sack of looted goods #7
Whiskey bottle #6
Cooked horse meat
3 Knives
3 Forks
3 Dinner Plates
Hardtack (3 pieces)
Whiskey bottle #7
Haggadah
strike on anything matches
Clean Bandages
Rucksack

Furniture/Set Dressing/Pre-Set Props
Whiskey bottle #1 (preset beneath floor boards)
Chair
Mattress
Chaise
Blankets
Quilts
Sacks with pilfered goods (2 and 3)
Candles
Chairs
Small pieces of furniture
Mounds of clothing

Saddle
Grandfather clock
Chandelier
Rolls of carpets
Paintings
Furniture
Stacks of silverware
Towers of books
Rocking horse
Children's toys
Stacks of silver serving pieces
Wooden boxes filled with random stolen items
Hurricane lamps
Seder table setting:

- 2 Candle Sticks w/Candles
- Lace tablecloth
- Whiskey Bottle (Special Occasion Decanter)
- Passover plate
- egg
- several collard green leaves
- shank bones
- Bowl with water
- Four glasses

COSTUME LIST

SIMON (worn through entire play)
Wool Vest
Shirt
Suspenders
Wool Trousers
Shoes
Overcoat
Hat
Shirt #2 (Rigged to Tear)

SIMON (Scene Four)
ADD: Yarmulke/Skullcap
ADD: Traveling greatcoat
ADD: Rain hat
ADD: Prosthetic Whipping Scar

CALEB (worn through entire play)
Confederate Kepi
Richmond Grey Shell Jacket
Grey Mounted Trousers
Suspenders
Distressed Shirt
Riding Boots
Bandages (with blood and dirt)
White & Blue Pillow Tick shirt
Trousers (rigged to tear)
Sling for "amputated" leg

CALEB (Scene Four)
ADD: Yarmulke/Skullcap

JOHN (Scene One)
Shirt (Distressed)
Trousers (Distressed, ripped hem)
Overcoat (Distressed)
Bandage for hand
Bowler (Distressed)
Burlap face mask

JOHN (Scenes Two, Three, and Four)
Black Lace-up Dress Shoes
Cotton Trousers
Suspenders
Pleated Front Cotton Dress Shirt

JOHN (Scene Four)
ADD: Yarmulke/Skullcap

From the Reviews of
THE WHIPPING MAN...

"A mesmerizing drama."
- Peter Filichia, *Newark Star-Ledger*

"A cause for celebration. Mathew Lopez has come as close as any author could to producing a microcosm of the genesis of a wide range of today's Black American males."
- Bob Rendell, *Talkin' Broadway*

"I can see why director Lou Bellamy chose this play for Penumbra, whose most famous alumnus is playwright August Wilson. In its complex welter of issues, in its interior explorations... *The Whipping Man* is Wilsonian."
- Rohan Preston, *Minneapolis Star-Ledger*

"Succeeds with an uncanny maturity in using sharply drawn characters and rich metaphor to wrestle Wilson-like with epic American issues of race, religion, and responsibility. Someone must succeed Wilson; it might as well be Lopez."
- Tim Gihring, *Minnesota Monthly*

Breinigsville, PA USA
24 January 2010
231288BV00004B/2/P

9 780573 697098